A Parade for Sam

Written by **Mary Labatt**

Illustrated by **Marisol Sarrazin**

Kids Can Press

Kids Can Read ™ Kids Can Read is a trademark of Kids Can Press Ltd.

Kids Can Press acknowledges the financial support of the Government of Ontario, through the Ontario Media Development Corporation's Ontario Book Initiative; the Ontario Arts Council; the Canada Council for the Arts; and the Government of Canada, through the BPIDP, for our publishing activity.

Published in Canada by
Kids Can Press Ltd.
29 Birch Avenue
Toronto, ON M4V 1E2

Published in the U.S. by
Kids Can Press Ltd.
2250 Military Road
Tonawanda, NY 14150

www.kidscanpress.com

Edited by David MacDonald
Designed by Marie Bartholomew
Printed and bound in China

The hardcover edition of this book is smyth sewn casebound.
The paperback edition of this book is limp sewn with a drawn-on cover.

CM 05 0 9 8 7 6 5 4 3 2 1
CM PA 05 0 9 8 7 6 5 4 3 2 1

Library and Archives Canada Cataloguing in Publication

Labatt, Mary, [date]

   A parade for Sam / written by Mary Labatt ; illustrated by Marisol Sarrazin.

(Kids Can read)
ISBN 1-55337-787-7 (bound).   ISBN 1-55337-788-5 (pbk.)

I. Sarrazin, Marisol, 1965– II. Title. III. Series: Kids Can read (Toronto, Ont.)

PS8573.A135P37 2005   jC813'.54   C2004-907372-9

Kids Can Press is a **Corus** ™ Entertainment company

Something went boom.

Rat-a-tat, rat-a-tat. Boom!

Sam ran to the window.

Rat-a-tat, rat-a-tat. Boom!

Sam ran to get Joan and Bob.

"Woof!" said Sam.

"Woof! Woof!"

"What is it, Sam?" asked Bob.

Joan opened the door.

Rat-a-tat, rat-a-tat. Boom!

"A parade!" said Joan.

"Let's go!" said Bob.

"Woof!" said Sam.

A girl with a baton came first.

Then came a big drum

and some little drums.

Rat-a-tat, rat-a-tat. Boom!

Boom went the big drum.

"I can do that!" thought Sam.

"Woof!" she said.

"Woof! Woof!"

A band played music.

"I can do that!" thought Sam.

"Aaa-ooo-oooooo," she said.

Next came big, big balloons.

Sam saw an elephant balloon,

a tiger balloon, a bear balloon

and a monkey balloon.

"I like parades!" thought Sam.

11

Next came the jugglers.

Sam saw fast jugglers, slow jugglers,

short jugglers and tall jugglers.

All the jugglers did tricks.

"I can do that," thought Sam,

and she jumped for a ball.

"Oh, no!" said a juggler.

"Get out of the parade, puppy!"

Next came the clowns.

Sam saw big clowns, small clowns,

short clowns and tall clowns.

All the clowns did tricks.

"I can do that!" thought Sam,

and she jumped for a hoop.

"Oh, no!" said a clown.

"Get out of the parade, puppy!"

Next came the dancers.

Sam saw fast dancers, slow dancers,

short dancers and tall dancers.

"I can do that!" thought Sam,

and she danced.

"Oh, no!" said a dancer.

"Get out of the parade, puppy!"

Joan grabbed Sam.

Sam wiggled,

but Joan held her tight.

"No," she said.

"Parades are not for puppies."

"Not for puppies!" thought Sam.

"Who says parades are not for puppies?

Look what is coming!"

Next came the dogs.

Sam saw big dogs, small dogs,

fat dogs and skinny dogs.

"Those are dogs!" thought Sam.

"I am a dog.

Parades ARE for puppies!"

All the dogs did tricks.

Sam wiggled and wiggled.

"I can do that," she thought.

"I am a dog, too!"

Sam wiggled out of Joan's arms.

She jumped in with the dogs.

"Woof!" said Sam.

"Woof! Woof!" said the dogs.

"Oh, no!" said the dog trainer.

"Get out of the parade, puppy!"

The dog trainer grabbed for Sam.

Joan grabbed for Sam.

Bob grabbed for Sam.

But Sam got away!

Sam ran past the dogs.

She ran past the dancers,

past the clowns,

past the jugglers,

past the band

and past the big drum.

"I do not want to watch the parade,"

thought Sam.

"I want to be IN the parade!"

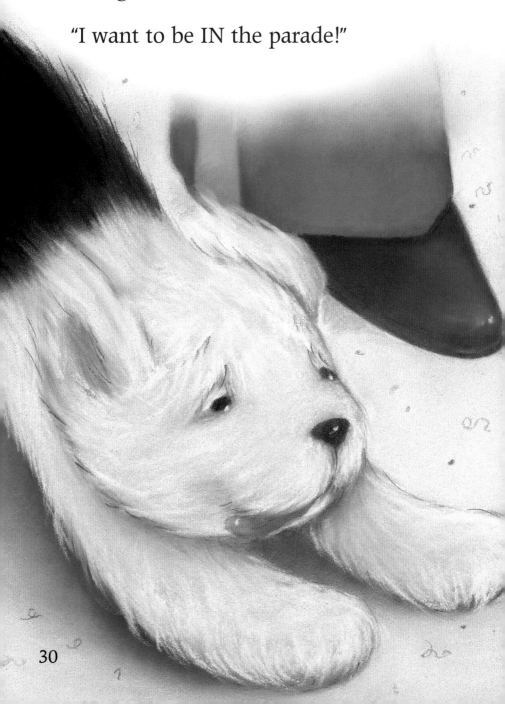

"Hello, puppy," said the

girl with the baton.

"Come with me!"

Boom went the big drum.

"Woof!" said Sam.

"Now the parade can follow ME!"